MS WIZ – MILLIONAIRE

Terence Blacker has been a full-time writer since 1983. In addition to the best-selling *Ms Wiz* stories, he has written a number of books for children, including the *Hotshots* series, *The Great Denture Adventure*, *The Transfer*, *Homebird* and *The Angel Factory*.

What the reviewers have said about *Ms Wiz*:

"Filled with the usual magic and mayhem, this book will be enjoyed by all Ms Wiz fans."
Books for Keeps

"Hilarious and hysterical."
Susan Hill, *Sunday Times*

"Terence Blacker has created a splendid character in the magical Ms Wiz. Enormous fun."
The Scotsman

"Sparkling zany humour . . . brilliantly funny."
Children's Books of the Year

Terence Blacker

Ms Wiz –
Millionaire

Illustrated by Tony Ross

MACMILLAN
CHILDREN'S BOOKS

First published 2001 by Macmillan Children's Books
a division of Macmillan Publishers Limited
20 New Wharf Road, London N1 9RR
Basingstoke and Oxford
www.panmacmillan.com

Associated companies throughout the world

ISBN 0 330 39731 1

1 3 5 7 9 8 6 4 2

A CIP catalogue record for this book is available from
the British Library.

Typeset by Intype London Ltd
Printed and bound in Great Britain by Mackays of Chatham plc, Kent

CHAPTER ONE

Chummy Lightfingers

Something rather odd was happening at St Barnabas School. It seemed to be disappearing. Bit by bit, day by day, there was less of it to see.

First a silver cup went missing from the school trophy cabinet in the hall. Then it was Miss Gomaz's cassette recorder. Then a painting from behind the headteacher's desk. Then a vacuum cleaner, three towels and 25 toilet rolls from the school store cupboard. Then the goalposts (with their nets) from the playground. Then Mr Bailey's brand-new mountain bike.

The caretaker Mr Brown started to stay late to keep guard on the school. New locks were bought. A light was set up in the playground. But nothing seemed to work.

Then, one night, the unthinkable happened. For several months, parents and teachers had been collecting money so that the school could buy a small playing-field that was for sale next door to it. Over £1,000 was being kept in a small security safe in a locked cupboard in the headteacher Mr Gilbert's office.

Until that too disappeared. When Mr Gilbert arrived at school one Monday morning, he found that the cupboard doors were open. The safe was gone.

Mr Gilbert was not a hasty man. Problems, he had found, quite often faded away if you did absolutely nothing about them.

But now everything else was fading away and it was the problem that was getting bigger. There was nothing for it. He was just going to have to take action. He lifted the phone on his desk and rang the local police station. "PC Boote, please," he said.

That morning, Mr Gilbert spoke to the entire school at morning Assembly. Behind him, sitting with the teachers, was the unmistakable figure of PC Boote, his peaked cap on his lap.

"Like any school, we have had our problems," Mr Gilbert said. "Problems in the classroom, problems in the playground, problems with school inspectors, problems on parents' evenings. Problems, problems, problems." He sighed and seemed to drift off into a daydream.

Behind him, Mrs Hicks cleared her throat loudly. Mr Gilbert started awake.

"Er, yes, sorry. Today we face the biggest problem I have experienced since arriving at St Barnabas. And I've decided . . . What have I decided?" He looked around helplessly. "I've decided to ask PC Boote to talk to you all." He sat down hurriedly.

The policeman walked slowly forward, put his cap on his head, and folded his arms in front of him as he looked around the hall.

"Morning, kids," he said quietly.

"Morning, PC Boote," replied the children in Assembly.

"You know, normally when I come down to see you at St Barnabas, it's to tell you about crossing the road safely – look right, left and right again – or not talking to the Danger Stranger or the importance of picking up your litter. But today I'm here to talk about something completely different." He paused dramatically. "I want to talk about nickers."

Several of the children laughed.

"By that I mean—" PC Boote seemed to be blushing "– people who are in the

habit of breaking and entering, doing a spot of half-inching and having it away on their toes before their collars can get felt. I am referring, of course, to our old friend Mr Chummy Lightfingers, your not-so-friendly local tea-leaf. Do I make myself entirely clear?"

"Er, no," someone in the front row muttered, just loud enough to hear.

"Nickers!" repeated PC Boote. "That is, people who nick things and get away with it – until now. The lads down at the station have come up with a plan – something that will catch this particular nicker red-handed." He returned to his seat and pulled out a heavy metal case from under the chair. "In this case are three security cameras which will film everything that happens at St Barnabas School, day and night." Glancing up at his audience, he clicked open the case and lifted the lid.

He looked down and stared into the

case. Then, as if not believing what he was seeing, he extended a hand and felt around inside it. Slowly, he stood up and, for a moment, seemed to be about to cry.

"All right then," he said. "Who's nicked my cameras?"

Jack Beddows and Lizzie Smith of Class Five stood gloomily outside the school hall. "I can't believe that there's someone who wants to steal things from our school," said Lizzie.

"Yeah." Jack glanced over to where PC Boote stood talking to Mr Gilbert. "And all we get is a policeman talking about nickers, Chummy Lightfingers, and then getting his own stuff stolen."

"Whoever the thief is, they must be pretty good," said Lizzie. "It's almost as if they're using magic."

The words seemed to hang in the air for a moment. Then, across the playground, a distant humming sound could be heard.

A black van, with the words *Wizard Security Agency* written in gold letters on the side, drew up outside the school gates. A woman in a trim, dark suit stepped out, pushed open the school gate and walked briskly across the playground.

"Is that who I think it is?" said Jack.

"And, if it is, why is she dressed like a businesswoman?" asked Lizzie.

Without a moment's hesitation, the woman approached Mr Gilbert and PC Boote.

"Can I help you?" asked Mr Gilbert impatiently.

"The name's Wiz – Ms Wiz ... private detective."

Jack and Lizzie smiled at one another.

"Wiz?" Mr Gilbert looked nervous. He had a few memories of Ms Wiz. Whenever she appeared at the school, things became even more difficult than they were usually. "I thought you had, er, retired."

"So did I," said Ms Wiz. "But life's been a bit quiet recently. And now there have been so many burglaries in the town that I decided that a bit of magic was needed. So I've gone into the crime-busting game."

"A crime-buster with black nail-varnish? I don't think so," chuckled PC Boote. "Leave it to the experts, lady."

"This police officer is absolutely right," said Mr Gilbert. "Magic's for kids. This is a problem for grown-ups." He looked up to see Jack and Lizzie casually standing nearby. "Jack, Lizzie. Please escort this visitor off the school premises," he said.

Jack and Lizzie followed Ms Wiz back to her van. "It's so unfair," said Lizzie.

"And stupid," said Ms Wiz. "Because it just so happens that I know the identity of the thief."

"How?" asked Jack.

Ms Wiz smiled knowingly. "I have my methods," she said, and reaching into the top pocket of her jacket, she took out a small, white plastic card and handed it to Jack. "This is what I call 'the Magic Revealer'. Hold it very still on the palm of your hand and you will see a photograph of your thief at work."

Jack looked down. "Er, it's blank," he said.

But, as Lizzie peered over his shoulder, a hint of colour began to appear on the white of the card. As the picture grew clearer, a small figure could be seen. It was taking a small security safe from the cupboard in Mr Gilbert's office.

Jack gasped. "It's Kevin Lightly," he said. "He's only just started school. He's in Class One with Mrs Hicks."

"I can't believe it," whispered Lizzie. "He's such a funny, shy little boy."

"He must be working for someone else," said Jack. "We can't report him to the police."

"Maybe we could just . . . talk to him," said Lizzie.

Ms Wiz took back the Magic Revealer and slipped it into her pocket. "My thoughts exactly," she said.

CHAPTER TWO

A Family Business

It was an evening like any other for the Lightly family. Dodgy Dave Lightly was on the sofa studying the instruction manual for some stolen security cameras. Across the room, his wife Anita the Cheater was sitting at a machine that printed fake £50 notes. And, on the floor, sat their only son Kevin, doing some homework his father had given him – practising how to open padlocks with a pin.

Dodgy Dave looked around him and smiled. "My little family," he said. "Other people might go out to the cinema or sit in front of the TV but the Lightlys make our own entertainment in the old-fashioned way – working at the family business." He sniffed, suddenly feeling rather emotional. "Makes you feel proud, don't it?"

Kevin looked up. "But why can't we do some other kind of work, Dad? When people ask me what you do, why do I always have to tell them you're in the removal business?"

"But it's true, love," said Anita. "Your dad does remove things – and very well too."

"I'm like Robin Hood," said Dodgy Dave. "I steal from the rich – that's everyone else – and give to the poor – that's us."

"Except nobody from St Barnabas is very rich," muttered Kevin.

"Don't be rude to your father," murmured Anita. "You're very lucky he spends time helping you learn a trade. You'll thank him when you grow up."

"But I don't want to be a thief," said Kevin. "I want to be a teacher."

Dodgy Dave and Anita the Cheater stared at their son in amazement. "Any more of that talk and I'll send you to your room," Dave said eventually. "You'll break your poor mother's heart, you will."

Just then, the doorbell rang. "Now who could that be?" said Dodgy Dave, casually throwing a blanket over the stolen goods on the sofa.

"Maybe it's the police," said Kevin nervously.

"Nah, they don't bother ringing – they just kick the door down," said Anita.

Dodgy Dave stood by the door. "Who is it, please?" he called out in his politest voice.

"The name's Wiz – Ms Wiz . . . neighbourhood advice officer," came the voice from outside. "I'm looking for the Lightly family."

"They moved a couple of months

ago," said Dodgy Dave, winking at
Anita. "I heard they emigrated to
Australia."

There was a moment's pause. Then,
as a faint humming noise could be
heard from outside, the lock on the door
drew back and the door slowly opened.
"Thank you so much," said Ms Wiz,
entering the room.

"Hey, that was good," said Dodgy
Dave, running his finger down the side
of the door. "Are you in the breaking
and entering business too?"

Without a word, Ms Wiz reached into
her top pocket for the Magic Revealer.
"My card," she said.

Dodgy Dave looked down at the card
in his hand. "It's blank," he said. "Hang
on, it's one of those joke cards. There's
a picture of someone coming up." He
squinted at it more closely. "It looks a
bit like our Kevin."

"It is Kevin," said Ms Wiz. "And

he's carrying the safe at St Barnabas."

Anita peered over her husband's shoulder. "Ah, look at him, the little mite," she said.

"Have you got another one of these?" asked Dodgy Dave. "Maybe we could get it framed."

Ms Wiz frowned. "Aren't you worried that your son has been photographed stealing a safe from his school?" she said.

"Kevin?" Dodgy Dave winked at his wife. "You can't prove nothing. He was with us all that evening, whichever evening it was. "

"That's right," said Anita. "It must have been the night his dear old grandma was here. We've got loads of witnesses."

"As it happens," said Ms Wiz. "I have decided not to hand this evidence over to the police. I wanted to come round here to talk to you about giving up all this thieving."

Anita looked puzzled. "Why would we want to do that, then?" she asked.

"Because it's wrong," said Ms Wiz firmly. "And because, if you go on doing it, you're all going to end up in jail."

"And because I don't like it," murmured Kevin under his breath.

"But—" Ms Wiz smiled. "I want to give you another chance. I believe that, given an opportunity in life, all of us are basically good."

"That's true enough," said Dodgy Dave. "I'm good at breaking and entering. Anita here's an artist when it comes to faking notes and Kevin's got lovely little fingers for opening locks—"

"Let me put it another way." Ms Wiz spoke more sharply. "I am a private paranormal detective. I have my methods. Because I have rather special, magical powers, I can produce evidence that other detectives can only dream of.

For example—" She reached into the leather bag at her feet, and took out a matchbox. "What would you say this is, Kevin?" She carefully opened the box.

"Ugh," said Kevin. "It seems to be a dead fly."

"Actually, it's a camera," said Ms Wiz. "I call this my 'Magic Visualiser'. I released it outside St Barnabas School. It followed you into the school when you broke in and photographed everything

you did. The result appears on the Magic Revealer. You see, with my paranormal powers, I can make things move, disappear—"

"We can all do that," said Dodgy Dave.

"I can even predict what's going to happen in the future." Ms Wiz took what seemed to be a small photograph frame out of her bag. "This is my Magic Predictor," she said. "It's like a video recorder, only it can film things which have yet to happen."

Dodgy Dave examined the frame thoughtfully. "That could be handy," he murmured.

"But if you promise to give up thieving, I won't hand over any of this evidence to PC Boote."

"Could you just show me how the Magic Predictor works?" Dodgy Dave wandered casually over to the television and switched it on. "For instance, could you predict what would be on this TV channel on Saturday evening at, say, eight o'clock?"

A faint humming sound filled the room and a small cloud of fog enveloped the Magic Predictor. When it cleared, a picture could be seen in the frame. "There you are," said Ms Wiz. "It seems to be some sort of game show. There are lots of little balls with numbers on them."

"Oh yes, so it is." Dodgy Dave picked up a pen and, staring at the frame, jotted something down on the back of his hand. "Thank you, Ms Wiz," he said, switching the television off. "You've really made me think about things." He stood up. "I've decided. I'm through with nicking things. We're all definitely going straight from now on."

"We are?" said Anita.

"Excellent," said Ms Wiz, returning the Magic Predictor to her bag. "I knew that, if we discussed all this in a civilised way, you'd see sense."

"And, goodness me, you were right," said Dodgy Dave. "You've certainly changed our lives, Ms Wiz. We'll return the stuff we took from St Barnabas during half-term."

"We will?" said Anita.

Dodgy Dave walked quickly to the door. "Thanks a bunch, then," he said.

"You're very welcome." Ms Wiz smiled. "Goodbye, Kevin. Goodbye, Mr and Mrs Lightly."

Nodding and smiling, Dodgy Dave closed the door behind Ms Wiz. He walked slowly back into the room. "She has changed our life an' all," he said, staring thoughtfully at the back of his hand.

"That Predictor thing was showing the National Lottery," said Kevin.

"That's right, son. And now I know the winning numbers."

"Oh, Dave." A smile came to Anita's

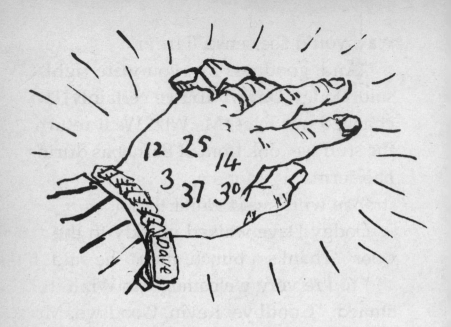

face. "You're a genius."

"All we need to do is buy a ticket for Saturday and we'll be made for life," chuckled Dodgy Dave. Soon Mr and Mrs Lightly were dancing around the room. "We're rich! We're rich!" they shouted.

From below the window, Ms Wiz heard the sounds of laughter. She looked up and smiled. "Another job well done," she said quietly.

CHAPTER THREE

The Fickle Finger of Fate

The following Monday, there were strange scenes outside St Barnabas School. Photographers lined the street, newspaper reporters with notebooks and tape recorders jostled at the gate to the playground where PC Boote was trying to keep order.

Everybody wanted to catch a glimpse of the winners of that weekend's fifteen million pound triple roll-over lottery, the Lightly family. The winners, Mr and Mrs Lightly, had not been seen in public but the rumour had spread that, on Monday morning, they would be taking their little boy Kevin to school as usual.

A surge of bodies towards the corner of the street was the first sign that the Lightlys were approaching. When they appeared, a crowd gathered round. Over the click and clatter of cameras, reporters shouted their questions.

"How are you feeling, Dave?"

"Which of you chose the lucky numbers?"

"What are you going to do with the money, Anita?"

"Give us a wave, Kevin!"

"Hold up, hold up." Dave Lightly raised both hands for silence. "At the end of the day, to be fair, it hasn't quite sunk in yet," he said. "But, as you can see, we're just an ordinary family taking our little lad to school. Just because I happen to have fifteen million quid in the bank, that doesn't change anything."

PC Boote pushed his way through the crowd. "Dodgy Dave Lightly, a millionaire – I've seen everything now," he murmured as he led the family towards the school gates.

Dodgy Dave smiled coldly. "It'll be

Mr Lightly from now on, thank you, Constable."

As Kevin Lightly entered the playground, he was immediately surrounded by children from Class One, laughing and congratulating him and asking him questions.

Jack and Lizzie paused to watch the scene.

"One day Ms Wiz pays a visit to the Lightly family. The following weekend, they win the lottery," Lizzie murmured.

"It could be a coincidence," said Jack.

They watched Kevin as he pushed through the crowd. As he passed them, he glanced in their direction, then looked away quickly.

"Something weird's going on here," said Lizzie. "I think we need to speak to that paranormal detective, don't you?"

*

But it was Ms Wiz who found them. That
afternoon, as Jack and Lizzie were
walking home after school, an extremely
unusual sight awaited them on the
High Street. A long, white limousine was
parked outside the chemist, the
newsagent, the fish and chip shop, and
the pub. Several people stood on the
pavement nearby, admiring the car and
peering through its darkened windows
to see who was inside.

As Jack and Lizzie passed, the limo seemed to purr into life. After a few moments, it moved forward at walking pace, staying a few metres behind them.

"Don't look now," murmured Lizzie. "But I think we're being followed by a giant car."

One of the car's windows opened slightly. "Want a lift, then?" said a woman's voice.

Lizzie glanced in the direction of the car. A hand was now beckoning through the window. Lizzie couldn't help noticing that on its fingers was black nail-varnish.

The car stopped and the third of three back doors opened to reveal, lounging on the back seat, the elegant figure of a woman in a blue silk dress. "The name's Wiz – Ms Wiz . . . millionaire," she said.

"What's going on, Ms Wiz?" asked Jack. "Where did you get this flash motor?"

"This is not so much a flash motor as a moving luxury home," said Ms Wiz.

When they stepped into the car, it was like entering a rather grand sitting-room. There were low lights all round. Soft music was playing in the background. In one corner, beside a large leather chair, was a table on which there were crisps and nuts and bottles of lemonade, while in another corner there was a TV.

Ms Wiz waved a hand in the direction of the table. "Help yourself to anything you like," she said.

"Hey, great spell, Ms Wiz," said Jack, settling into one of the chairs.

"It is rather magical, isn't it?" said Ms Wiz. "But it's not a spell. Kevin's dad, that dear Mr Lightly, gave me a few pounds – well, a couple of million pounds to be precise – to thank me, and I thought I'd give myself a treat. I don't like champagne. I can't stand shopping. But I just love cars. So I got the very biggest one I could find and hired myself a chauffeur." She lifted the receiver of a white telephone from the wall beside her. "We'll just drive around for a while. Yes—" Ms Wiz's smile became a little forced. "I know that's what we've been doing all day but we're going to do it a bit more."

"What exactly was Kevin's dad thanking you for?" asked Lizzie.

"For saving him from a life of crime. I went to the Lightlys' flat, talked to them about what a good thing honesty was and he said, 'Fine, OK, Ms Wiz.' And that was that."

"And three days later, he won the lottery," said Lizzie.

"Yes." Ms Wiz laughed. "The fickle finger of fate. Isn't it marvellous? By the way, what exactly is a lottery?"

Jack and Lizzie glanced at one another. "It's where lots of people buy a ticket with six numbers and the winning numbers are announced on a TV show every week."

"On TV." Ms Wiz looked thoughtful. "Would that be on a Saturday night?"

"That's the main one," said Lizzie.

"So if someone had a Magic Predictor, which told the future, they might be able to—"

"Oh, Ms Wiz," groaned Jack. "What have you done?"

"Could we see this Magic Predictor?" asked Lizzie.

"Bit of a problem there," said Ms Wiz quietly. "The old magic doesn't seem to be working quite so well this week. In fact, it's not working at all."

There was a brief silence in the car. "What about the spells?" said Jack. "The FISH powder? The Mickey Mouse alarm clock/time machine." A sudden thought occurred to him. "What about Herbert, the magic rat?"

"Oh, he's fine." Ms Wiz reached into the sleeve of her dress and carefully took out a brown and white rat. "Only he can't talk any more. He's – well, he's just a normal rat."

"Normal? Herbert? I don't believe it," said Lizzie.

Ms Wiz shrugged and looked away. "Who needs magic when you've got

loads of money?"

"D'you remember the first time you came to St Barnabas?" Jack asked suddenly. "You told us that magic should never be used for personal greed. Now Kevin's dad has won the lottery thanks to your magic and you're driving around in a big car – that's why your spells don't work any more."

"You win some, you lose some." Ms Wiz laughed nervously. "Thank

goodness that, although I now have a
huge fortune, I'm just the same old me."

Jack and Lizzie looked more closely
at Ms Wiz. She seemed to have done
something fluffy and expensive to her
hair and was definitely wearing more
make-up than she ever used to. There
was a strange, empty look to her green
eyes.

"Yes," said Jack uncertainly. "Thank
goodness for that."

"What about the Lightlys?" asked
Lizzie. "Have they changed?"

"Only for the better," said Ms Wiz.
"David has told me that he's going to
give lots of money to good causes. They
live on the top floor of the Grand Hotel
now. In fact, I'm going round for tea
tomorrow. David said that we
millionaires should stick together.
Maybe you'd like to see them too."

Jack glanced at Lizzie. "I think that
would be an excellent idea," he said.

CHAPTER FOUR

The Same, Only Much Richer

When the lift opened on the top floor of the Grand Hotel the next day, Ms Wiz, Jack and Lizzie found that a butler was waiting for them. He seemed to be swaying slightly.

"Would you be Mish—" He closed his eyes and shook his head. "Mishter Lightly's tea guests?" he asked in a low, slurred voice.

"That's us," said Ms Wiz brightly.

"Step this way, please." The butler turned and walked slowly down the corridor, occasionally bouncing off the walls.

"I think he must be drunk," whispered Lizzie.

"Nonsense," said Ms Wiz. "That's

probably just the way he walks."

At the end of the corridor was a pair of large double doors. Holding on to the two golden door-handles and resting his head against the door, the butler intoned, "And who shall I shay ish calling?"

"We are Ms Dolores Wisdom, Mr Jack Beddows and Miss Elizabeth Smith," said Ms Wiz in her poshest voice.

The butler leant forward and opened the door, losing his balance briefly. He took a deep breath and announced, "Ms Jack Wizzo, Mr Brenda Toes and Elish . . . Elish Whatshername." Then he stepped aside with a low bow and, in this position, backed out of the door behind them.

Ms Wiz, Jack and Lizzie were in a big, high-ceilinged room. Through a haze of cigar smoke, four men could be seen sitting at a table in the middle of the room, playing cards.

One of the men looked in their direction. "Well, if it isn't good old Ms Wiz," he said. "Come to join the party, then?"

"Hello, David," said Ms Wiz with a polite, strained smile. "You invited me to tea. I took the liberty of bringing along Jack and Lizzie from Kevin's school."

"Tea? You're having a laugh!" Dave's voice echoed around the room. "Nobody drinks tea round here. It's champagne all the way."

Ms Wiz glanced at the floor which was strewn with empty bottles. "So I see," she said.

"Want to join us, then? The kids can go and see Kevin – he's just down the corridor, playing with his new, *stonkingly* expensive computer."

"I'm not a gambler myself." Ms Wiz walked slowly towards the table. "So this is what you do all day since you won the lottery. You haven't helped any good causes at all."

"Course I have." Dodgy Dave chuckled. "I'm buying a football club. I'm looking very seriously at a tropical island in the Pacific. I'm giving my mates a good time, aren't I, lads?"

"Diamond geezer, old Dave," said one of the men. "Yeah, heart of gold," said another. The third seemed to have fallen asleep, his head on the table.

"Then there's my family." Dodgy Dave stood up and walked towards a side door. "They're another good cause." He opened the door. Anita Lightly was reclining on a giant bed in a pink silk dressing-gown. A young man was manicuring her toenails while she thumbed through a catalogue, a pen in her hand. "Once she used to work all day at her printing business. Now she can do all her shopping without getting out of bed. That's a good cause in anyone's language."

He closed the door and walked down
a corridor to another side-room. Ms
Wiz, Jack and Lizzie looked through the
door to see three of the children from
Class One in front of a giant computer
screen. Kevin Lightly stood behind
them, watching as they played. "Ever
since he got that computer, he's the
most popular kid in his class," said
Dodgy Dave. At that moment, Kevin
looked up and waved, unsmilingly.

"He doesn't seem to be having much fun himself," said Lizzie.

Dodgy Dave shrugged. "He's gone a bit quiet ever since we became millionaires. I expect it's the excitement."

"But when you were talking to those reporters, you said you were just an ordinary family and that being a multimillionaire wasn't going to change you," said Jack.

"It hasn't," said Dodgy Dave cheerfully. "We're just the same, only much, much richer. We've got ourselves a new hobby – spending loads of money."

Ms Wiz put her arm round Dodgy Dave's shoulders. "David," she said in a quiet, dangerous voice. "Do you remember when we first met I told you that I was a paranormal detective?"

Dodgy Dave nodded.

"Well, my special, paranormal powers

are telling me that you have used my magic to win the lottery." She stood back and raised both her hands. "And what magic can give, magic can take away."

At that moment, a faint humming noise could be heard in the room. As it grew louder, Ms Wiz closed her eyes, and clenched her fists. "Please. *Please*," she whispered. But, after a few seconds her shoulders slumped and the sound faded. For a moment, there was silence in the room.

"Who *is* this nutter?" said one of the men sitting at the table.

Ms Wiz looked around the room. "Gone," she whispered. "The magic's gone." Then, with a little sob, she ran to the double doors.

When Jack and Lizzie found her, she was standing by the lift, her face buried in her hands.

"Are you all right, Ms Wiz?" Lizzie placed a hand on her shoulder.

"It's all over. I've lost my powers."
Ms Wiz looked up and there were tears
in her eyes. "What am I going to do?"

The following day, Jack Beddows
arrived at St Barnabas School with a
plan. It wasn't a great plan. It was a plan
that could very easily go horribly
wrong. But he and Lizzie had agreed
that it was the only plan they could

think of which had a chance of bringing magic back into the life of Ms Wiz.

For the plan to have any chance of success, they needed the help of Kevin Lightly.

At first, when Jack and Lizzie explained what he would have to do, Kevin was reluctant. Then Jack and Lizzie told him of some of their magical adventures with Ms Wiz in the past – about travelling back in time and rescuing Jack, about saving Podge from becoming a zombie slave in the underworld, about Archimedes the mathematical barn owl and Herbert the magic rat.

"That Magic Visualiser of hers was pretty good," Kevin looked thoughtful. "And the Magic Predictor was amazing."

"But unless we do something, there will be no more spells because the golden rule about magic is that it must

never be used for selfish purposes,"
said Jack.

"Ms Wiz has said she's going to give
everything away, even her car," said
Lizzie. "But while your dad's still a
millionaire, she's helpless."

Kevin looked at them in
astonishment. "You want us to give all
our money away?"

"It's not as if it has made you any
happier," said Lizzie.

"Even Mum says she's bored of lying
around all day," Kevin said quietly. "It'll
be good if life could go back to the way
it was, but with Dad and Mum doing
normal jobs. But how would we do it?"

"All we need is a bit of inside
information." Jack smiled. "And you
can leave the rest to us."

CHAPTER FIVE

The Magic Truth-Teller

Mr Gilbert was in an excellent mood. Thanks to his talk to the school, all the stolen property (except for a few toilet rolls) had been returned during half-term. And now, it looked as if St Barnabas was going to be able to buy the playing-field next door.

He sat at his desk, remembering how Jack Beddows and Lizzie Smith of Class Five had told him that Mr Lightly was interested in giving the final £10,000 to the school on the condition that there would be a big presentation to mark the handing over of the money.

He had invited parents, some local reporters, even PC Boote to today's Assembly. He had even agreed to Jack's suggestion that Ms Wiz would put on a magic show for the children of the school.

He stood up and rubbed his hands. Mrs Gilbert would be proud of the way he had sorted out the school's problems. It was time for Assembly.

"Today is a very special day for St Barnabas School." Mr Gilbert stood before the entire school, then smiled at his guests of honour who were sitting in the front row.

"It's special," the headteacher continued, "because, at long last, the school will be able to have its own playing-field, thanks to a magnificent gesture by our most famous parents, Mr and Mrs Lightly."

To deafening applause, Dodgy Dave and Anita stood up. "Too kind, too kind," said Anita, curtseying one way then the other. "You're very welcome," said Dodgy Dave, a large cigar clamped between his teeth.

As the clapping died down, Dodgy Dave picked up the suitcase that was under his chair and stepped forward. "I thought of giving the school a cheque for the money but in the end I thought you'd like to see some real money." He opened the case to reveal that it was neatly packed with crisp £50 notes.

"Goodness, look how new these notes are," said Mr Gilbert. "It's as if they've just been printed."

"Eh?" A look of alarm crossed Dodgy Dave's face. "Er, yes, I collected them from the bank this morning."

"Perhaps you'd like to give a little message of inspiration to the children," said the headteacher.

Dodgy Dave thought for a moment, then took a step forward. "Kids," he said solemnly. "I want you all to know

that, at the end of the day, to be fair, money isn't everything. What matters in this world is not money itself – but what money can buy you. Big cars, for instance. Houses with jacuzzis on every floor. Mink fur coats for the wife. Holidays in very sunny places. And above all—" He hesitated and seemed to be overcome with emotion. "Quality time, every day of the week, to play cards with your best mates."

As Dodgy Dave swaggered back to his seat, Mr Gilbert seemed briefly to be lost for words. "Er, thank you, Mr Lightly, for those thoughts," he said. "And to mark the occasion, at the special request of Class Five, we have invited the one and only Ms Wiz to show us some of her famous magic spells."

Dodgy Dave leant over to Anita. "I thought that woman's magic didn't work any more," he murmured.

To cheers from the children, Ms Wiz

appeared from behind a curtain. In her hand, she held a small plastic wand. "Behold a special wand which I call 'the Magic Truth-Teller'," she said.

"Oh yeah?" Anita giggled. "I saw those wands being sold down the market yesterday."

"The Magic Truth-Teller has the power to tell what is real from what is false. Only if something is not entirely genuine will the red light at the end light up."

She advanced on the front row and touched Anita's fur coat. Nothing happened to the wand. "That's real fur," said Ms Wiz.

"Shame," said Katrina rather loudly from the back.

Ms Wiz touched the ring on Anita's finger. Again, the wand remained the same. "Congratulations," said Ms Wiz. "That's a real diamond."

"What d'you expect?" muttered

Dodgy Dave.

Ms Wiz walked back to the front of the Assembly. As if noticing the case full of money for the first time, she clicked it open and, before Dodgy Dave could stop her, laid the wand on the notes inside. The red light lit up immediately. "Oh dear," said Ms Wiz. "The Magic Truth-Teller is revealing that there's something not quite right about these notes."

"Hello hello hello." PC Boote sat forward, suddenly interested.

"It's a bloomin' wind-up." Dodgy Dave laughed nervously. "She's pressing a button on the wand. She's the one that's fake."

But Ms Wiz had produced a picture-frame from her bag. "This looks like a normal frame, doesn't it? In fact, it's a Magic Predictor." She smiled down at the front row. "Isn't it, David?"

"I've warned you," said Dodgy Dave

between his teeth.

"It can reveal the future, of course –
but it can also reveal the past." Ms Wiz
put the frame on a table. "Let's look at
some scenes from the past of our special
guests," she said. "Shall we say, the
evening they decided to buy their
winning lottery ticket. Or the night last
September when there was a break-in
at the post office on the High Street."

"How did she know about that?"

Dodgy Dave whispered to Anita.

"But first of all we're going to see Mrs Lightly at work on her special printing machine."

There was a scream from Anita. "Stop her, Dave," she shouted.

Dodgy Dave stepped forward and put an arm round Ms Wiz's shoulders. "Great magic show, Ms Wiz," he said loudly, then whispered in her ear, "Are you mad? What are you trying to do to me?"

"Give all your money to charity and

I'll stop now," said Ms Wiz in a low voice.

A moan of despair came from Dodgy Dave. "How about half?" he murmured through the side of his mouth.

Ms Wiz shrugged herself free. "On with the show," she said.

"No!" He turned to the audience, a desperate, fixed grin on his face. "I've just made a very big decision, ladies and gentlemen," he said in a strangled voice. "I'm through with money. I'm going to give it all away."

There was a gasp from around the hall. "Dodgy Dave giving away money?" muttered PC Boote. "Something very funny's going on here."

"It's only cash, after all." With a trembling hand, Dodgy Dave took out a chequebook, wrote on it and gave it to Ms Wiz. "Here's a blank cheque made out to the school," he said. "You can do what you like with it." He snapped the suitcase shut. "Come on, love, let's go home." Grabbing Anita by the hand, he scurried out of the hall.

For a moment, there was silence. Smiling, Ms Wiz gave the cheque to Mr Gilbert. "A donation to good causes," she said. "And I can't think of a better cause than a playing-field for the children of St Barnabas."

Cheers echoed around the hall.

"Well," Mr Gilbert stared nervously at the cheque, "I said today would be special and I think it was. Er, wasn't it?"

After the Assembly had dispersed, Jack and Lizzie found Ms Wiz in the playground, talking to Kevin Lightly.

"Great magic show, Ms Wiz," said Jack.

Ms Wiz smiled at Kevin. "It's amazing what a plastic wand, an old picture frame and a bit of inside information can do," she said.

"Will Mum and Dad go back to nicking things like they used to?" Kevin asked.

"Not now that they know the power of magic," said Ms Wiz.

"That's all very well," said Lizzie. "But what about your own magic?"

Ms Wiz was about to reply when a familiar voice came from her bag. "Golly gosh and jimminy." Herbert the rat peered out. "I've just had the most

awful dream. I was a normal rat. The *embarrassment*, my dear."

"Don't think about it, Herbert," said Ms Wiz, turning towards the gate.

"Excuse me, miss." They turned to see the figure of PC Boote approaching. "Do you happen to be in possession of information about Mr and Mrs Lightly which could be of assistance to the police?" he asked.

Ms Wiz glanced at Kevin. "Only that they've generously given all their money to good causes," she said.

"Hmm." PC Boote looked unconvinced. "If I were you, I'd stick to magic and leave the crime-busting to the experts," he said, putting away his notebook.

Ms Wiz smiled. "I think that's the best advice I've had in a long time," she said.